Greek Entomyth-ology

written
& illustrated
by
Artemis Ippotis

My grateful thanks to all those who helped me to compile this book, but especially to
my husband Rodney
for his helpful suggestions and edits
&
my family & friends,
who thought me quite mad, but good-naturedly posed for me anyway!
& to Simon Munnery for his help and encouragement.

My hope is, that in addition to familiarising readers with the common Greek myths, this book will make them more
aware of all the variety of weird and wonderful creatures which inhabit our beautiful planet with us, which are
so crucial to our ecosystems, and thus to our survival.

Please note that, relative to one another, the insects are
NOT TO SCALE

10% of any profits will be donated to Wikipedia

Insect identification Consultant: Roger Key
Reference aids: DK Pocket book: Insects & Spiders; Collins Gem Butterflies & Moths;
Wikipedia; The Orchard Book of GREEK MYTHS

Order this book online at www.trafford.com
or email orders@trafford.com

Most Trafford titles are also available at major online book retailers.

© Copyright 2010 Artemis Ipotis.
All rights reserved. No part of this publication may be reproduced, stored in a retrieval system, or
transmitted, in any form or by any means, electronic, mechanical, photocopying, recording, or
otherwise, without the written prior permission of the author.

Printed in Victoria, BC, Canada.

ISBN: 978-1-4269-0050-1 (sc)

*Our mission is to efficiently provide the world's finest, most comprehensive book publishing
service, enabling every author to experience success. To find out how to publish your book, your
way, and have it available worldwide, visit us online at www.trafford.com*

Trafford rev. 6/7/2010

Trafford PUBLISHING www.trafford.com

North America & international
toll-free: 1 888 232 4444 (USA & Canada)
phone: 250 383 6864 • fax: 812 355 4082

Contents

ARACHNE..Page 1

ATALANTA's RACE..Page 4

DAPHNE & APOLLO...Page 5

DEMETER & PERSEPHONE......................................Page 6

ECHO & NARCISSUS..Page 12

(The twelve labours of) HERACLES..........................Page 14

ICARUS..Page 30

MIDAS..Page 32

ORPHEUS & EURYDICE..Page 35

PANDORA('s box)..Page 41

(pardoning)PROMETHEUS.......................................Page 44

PERSEUS..Page 46

SISYPHUS...Page 53

THESEUS..Page 55

Sue & Clive

With all good wishes
love from
Diana

Aka Artemis Ippotis

ARACHNE THE SPINNER

Arachne the spinner was known to be
Most awesomely good at tapestry ~
A maiden productive
With cloths so seductive,
She boasted "No-one is as good as me!"

"The gods made you skillful, most certainly",
Said tailors and weavers who came to see
If all this kerfuffle
About some maid's shuttle
Was everything it was cracked up to be.....

"What rubbish!" Arachne cried, haughtily ~
The gods have got NOTHING they can teach ME!
'Cos I can weave better
Than anyone yet - a
Contention I'll demonstrate, willingly!"

Her friends were alarmed, and said "Hush, my dear ~
The goddess Athene might overhear!"
But she was defiant,
On her skill reliant,
She answered, "Just what have I got to fear?"

Just then an old maid who'd been standing by
Came forward to ask her to clarify ~
"So you are believing
That your skill at weaving
Would beat any goddesses in the sky?"

"They don't stand a chance!" claimed our heroine ~
"I know that there's no-one who could out-spin
My intricate stitches ~
Such colourful riches
Mean that in a test I'd be BOUND to win!"

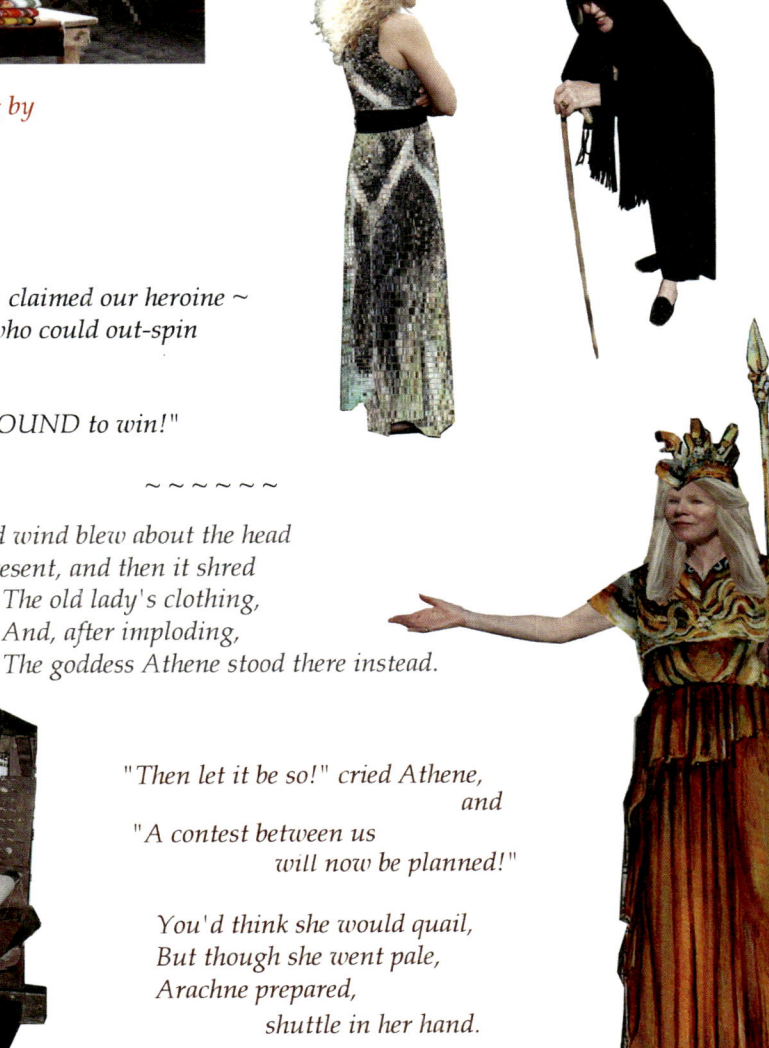

~ ~ ~ ~ ~ ~

Just then a cold wind blew about the head
Of everyone present, and then it shred
The old lady's clothing,
And, after imploding,
The goddess Athene stood there instead.

"Then let it be so!" cried Athene,
                              and
"A contest between us
         will now be planned!"

You'd think she would quail,
But though she went pale,
Arachne prepared,
         shuttle in her hand.

1

Back and forth their fingers flew,
    And from each loom such fabrics grew
        That all who witnessed were in awe
            Of those bright swatches that they saw.

The picture that Athene wove
Of gods and goddesses who strove
To be examples to mankind,
And were heroic, brave and kind,
Portrayed them in a gracious light,
And was a most inspiring sight.

Arachne, though, had used her tools
To cast the gods as silly fools,
Who lazed,
    and bragged.
        and drank,
            and fought,
And did things that they didn't ought.

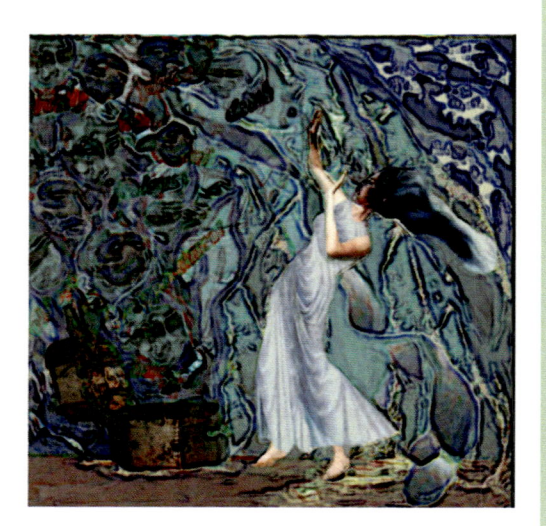

Throughout she weaved each blade of grass ~
Her sea-scapes shimmered like a glass,
And animals had fur-appeal ~
    So tactile that they could be real........

More brilliant
    in every way
Than real life,
    she wove that day.

So, when the contest
    stopped at last,
Arachne knew she
    had surpassed
Athene's tapestry,
    and grinned,
Most satisified
    with what
        she'd spinned.

"You are the winner, I admit,"
Athene said, on viewing it.
           "I told you so!" Arachne said,
           The triumph going to her head.

Athene paused, and gave a frown,
This upstart must be taken down!
    Such cheekiness could not be borne ~
    Of that smug smile she should be shorn!
    "In spite of all that matchless skill
    There's one thing that is greater still ~

And that's your vanity my dear ~
Perhaps you thought I wouldn't care
When you decide to ridicule
The gods, and make them play the fool?
Now pay attention one and all,
For pride will come before a fall.

She stepped towards Arachne and
She grabbed the shuttle from her hand ~
She said: "I'll teach you not to gloat!"
And **thrust** the shuttle down her throat!
Then, much to everyone's surprise,
Arachne changed before their eyes!
    Her body shrank, her fingers grew,
    Her arms stuck to her sides like glue.
    Down, down she went, until she got
    No bigger than a small ink-blot,
    And from her mouth still hung a twine
    Left over from her work so fine,

    The goddess used that silken thread
    Which still protruded from her head
    To leave her dangling from a tree
    ~ "For ever spin your tapestry!" ~
    The goddess cried, "But from now on,
   When people see the work you've done
  They'll shudder, and they'll tear it down,
And sweep you out of house and home.

Poor fair Arachne!
      Doomed to be
Forever
    weaving patiently!
Yet never more to be
        admired
By folk
   whose work
      she had *inspired!*

And to this day
    a spider's seen
As something that
      can make you
        SCREAM!

              But, if you look
                 more carefully,
             You'll marvel
                at her artistry,
           The intricacy of the web
           She spins,
              whilst hanging
                from that thread.
And maybe you'll believe 'tis so,
Arachne's PRIDE
          brought her this low.

Index : Garden Cross Spider (*Araneus Diadematus*)

ATALANTA'S RACE

Once, on the island of Cyprus, there lived a lovely maid,
Who swore she never would marry, and would not be gainsaid.
She was the King's only daughter, so this caused quite a stir,
And all the young men grew tiresome, they really pestered her. 
Until at last she grew weary, "Enough of all this strife!
If you can beat me at running then I will be your wife.
But if you lose in this contest you'll have to pay the price;
The penalty for your failure is that you'll lose your life!"

So many young men died trying, for she was very fast,
With long legs and tresses flying, no suitor could get past.
A young man called Hippomenes, heard this event regaled,
And felt most frightfully scornful of those who tried and failed.
"Well how incredibly stupid, to risk your life that way,
I would never do such a thing, that's all I have to say!"

But then when he got to know her he had to change his mind,
For she was sweet and beautiful, and talented, and kind.
"I'd rather die than not have her!" he pleaded with the King,
Although the King was reluctant to let him do this thing.

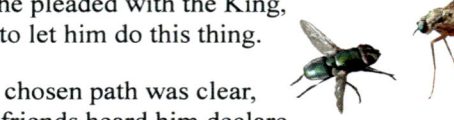

But he could not be deflected, his chosen path was clear,
"I'll either win, or die trying," his friends heard him declare.

He went to ask Aphrodite how he could win the race,
And she said, "Really it's simple, you have to slow her pace;
So take these three golden apples and throw them past her head,
And as she bends down to collect them you take the lead instead."

So young Hippomedes entered the race that risked his life
But thought that it was all worth it to win her for his wife.
He threw the bait as instructed, so Atalanta paused;
And as she did so, he passed her (which gathered some applause)
At last, with apples in both hands she went to get the third,
And as she stooped to collect it the watching crowd all cheered.
Hippomenes sprinted past her, he gave it all his best,
And hurled himself past the finish, lungs bursting in his chest.

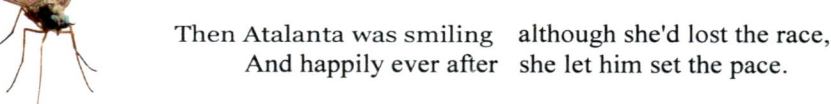

Then Atalanta was smiling although she'd lost the race,
And happily ever after she let him set the pace.

DAPHNE & APOLLO

It's never a good idea to ridicule a god,
(Or, for that matter, anyone whose path you have not trod)
One day the sun-god Apollo observed a tiny boy
With a tiny bow-and-arrow which looked just like a toy.
"Babies like you shouldn't meddle with weaponry of war!"
The fact Apollo was laughing made young god Eros sore.
"For that, I'll teach him a lesson!" exclaimed the young upstart,
And shot out a gold-tipped arrow which hit him in the heart.

Just then a beautiful naiad* had chanced to wander by,
Who went by the name of Daphne; Apollo heaved a sigh;
For though he was quite the darling of maidens everywhere,
For he was so tall and handsome, and talented, and fair,
He never before had wanted to win a a lady love,
But DAPHNE became his passion, his dear, his turtle dove.

Alas! Young Eros was watching, and drew a second dart,
Which flew through the air and shivvered right into Daphne's heart.
This time, instead of being golden, the tip was made of lead,
And from that ill-fated moment her heart was filled with dread.
This made her respond with horror to his advances, so
She sprinted away in terror~ she didn't want to know.

Apollo went chasing after, up hill and over dale
And as he drew ever nearer poor Daphne grew quite pale;

At last it seemed he would catch her ~so Daphne gasped a prayer,
"Oh save me please, Father River, he has me by the hair!"
So saying, her feet sank into the earth, and took root there.

"I've got you at last!" Apollo declared triumphantly;
But he was brought up abruptly~ his arms wrapped round a tree.
For Daphne was turned to laurel, her tears were falling leaves,
Her arms were two graceful branches which swayed upon the breeze.

"I only wanted to love you!" he cried out painfully,
"But though you won't be my lover I'll serve you faithfully."

And from that day all the heros returning from the wars,
And Kings and Emp'rors and sportsmen who got the highest scores,
Were crowned with a wreath of laurels to keep her memory.
Apollo declared bay laurel to be a sacred tree.

*water-nymph

DEMETER & PERSEPHONE

In summer when the sun is high
You'll see the comma butterfly.
This butterfly looks like a leaf,
But if you study underneath
You'll find there is a question mark
Which has it's origins in dark
Events that took place long ago,
Before the world had learned to snow;
And this is how that came about,
The ancient legend spells it out..........

Once upon a long-ago
It didn't hail, it didn't snow,
And Mother Earth was never blue
For it was summer all year through.
A goddess tended countryside,
And spread her bounty far and wide.

Demeter was her name, and she
Had daughter called Persephone.
By nature sweet and dutiful,
Persephone the beautiful.
The apple of her mother's eye,
She made the sunny days fly by.

Now Hades, King of all the dead,
Who lived in Underworld so dread,
Where sunshine never found it's way,
And night-time reigned instead of day,
Was cold and lonely as could be:~
He longed for female company.

He sometimes ventured out to see
The young girls, playing prettily,
And though the bright light hurt his eyes,
He risked it all, to hear their sighs,
And see the way they played about,
So free from misery and doubt.

Index : Comma butterfly, Speckled wood butterfly,
Mole cricket (m) , Red Admiral butterfly & Painted lady butterfly

6

One day he spied Persephone
Who gathered violets by a tree.
"She is the one!" he cried in glee,
"Oh yes! She is the one for me!"
And harnessing his trusty steed
He thundered out to do the deed.

He lashed his whip, and rode full tilt,
And all the earth began to wilt.
His wheels felled trees to left and right,
And nature shook with shock and fright.
Then, holding reins aside, caught fair
Persephone by her long hair.

Index: Comma butterfly
       Devil's coach horse beetle
       Mole cricket (m)

"Oh let me go! Leave me alone!"
Persephone began to moan;
"Oh save me won't you, Mother dear?"
Alas! Her mother couldn't hear.
A gaping chasm opened then,
And down they fell to Hades' den.

"Don't cry!" said Hades, "You will be
My queen, and reign down here with me,
And all the riches of the earth
I give to you, for what that's worth."

But she just sobbed and gave a groan,
"I want my Mother! Take me home!"

So when they reached the river Styx
Which runs above/below betwixt
She cried "Oh river, pity me!
And save me, I'm Persephone!"
The river tried to trip the god
But he just kicked it like a dog.

Then in despair Persephone
Untied her wreath and cast it free
To show her mother she was there
Before being captured by her hair.
She bad the river bear her twine
As silent witness to this crime.

Demeter's mind was in a whirl -
She HAD to find her darling girl!
But she had simply disappeared -
No sign at all! - how very weird!
But then she spied the garland near
The river-bank, and shed a tear.

The water whispered in her ear -
"She's in the UNDERWORLD my dear,
For HADES stole her by her hair
And carted her off down to there,
To be his queen, and reign with him
In that dread place so dark and grim."

Demeter went demented then,
And raced up to the gates of
    heav'n,
She rattled at them,
    shouting "ZEUS!"
My daughter's gone! There's
    NO EXCUSE
For Hades' act, so GET HER
    BACK,
Or I will pine, and earth
    will lack!"

Author's note: Hades was sometimes known as Pluoto: hence the Romans called him Pluto.

Zeus heaved a sigh, and pulled a face,
But rules are rules, and in this case
The rule was that Persephone
Must not EAT anything while she
Was in the Underworld, for then
She had to STAY in Hades' den.

Demeter understood her plight,
Beseeching Zeus with all her might -
"Then put your MESSENGER to flight
To WARN her NOT TO TAKE A BITE!
You ARE the ruler, after all,
And other gods are in your thrall!"

So Zeus sent Hermes with all speed
Although Demeter took the lead;
She hurried him and pulled his sleeve
She was so anxious to retrieve
Her captured daughter
from that Lord,
The god of all
the Underworld.

Meanwhile,
on weary earth below,
Fell a first covering
of snow,
And all the trees lay
cold and bare
Because they lacked
Demeter's care.

Index:
Luber Grasshopper
Comma Butterfly
Dragonfly (Migrant Hawker)

9

Now Hades, getting in his stride,
Prepared a feast for his new bride,
With starter, main courses, and sweet -
"Come on, my dear, you HAVE to eat!"
So hungry was Persephone
That she was tempted, he could see........
He put twelve seeds in front of her -
"Twelve seeds can't harm you,
                               you'll concur?"

Just then came skimming through the air
Hermes the wingèd messenger -
"Oh noble Hades! Zeus commands
That you accede to her demands
And free her from this dire fate -
Or have I just arrived too late?"

"Yes!" cried Hades, "She has eaten!
Zeus and Demeter are beaten!"

Persephone cried out in fear -
"What DO you mean, what's this I hear?"
As six small pomegranate pips
She snatched back from her trembling lips.

"You rascal, Hades! You were cruel
To not give warning of the rule!
But, I suppose, it is too late -
Those six small seeds have sealed her fate!"

"I HATE you!" cried Persephone,
And ALWAYS WILL, you wait and see!"

Then Hades pleaded, "Don't you know
How LONELY I'll be if you go?"
So Hermes said "Let Zeus decide!"
And, as he really loved his bride
Great Hades said he would agree
To Zeus's judgement and decree.

Then Zeus decided, to be fair,
His judgement was that they should share,
And for six months Persephone
Could roam the earth, at peace and free,
But in the autumn she must go
Back to the Underworld below.

And so it came that gradually,
As time went by, Persephone
Began to love her husband, though
She really missed her mother so.

And up on earth Demeter grieves
And trees flush red, and drop their leaves,
And flowers wither, crops don't grow.
And in the winter, it will snow.

But come the spring, her duty done
Persephone will bring warm sun,
Throughout the land Demeter and
Persephone flit hand-in-hand.
As all of nature they entrance
The birds will sing, and creatures dance.

So in the winter when you try
To spot the comma butterfly
You may mistake it for a leaf
As it will hibernate beneath
The hedgerow, waiting for the day
Persephone returns to play......

11

ECHO & NARCISSUS

On Mount Olympus, where the goddesses all played,
Chasing the deer through quiet woods of dappled shade,
Queen Hera, silent as the golden rays of sun,
Artemis, moving like moonbeams, who could out-run
The fastest deer, and wood-nymphs who would softly dance
About the trees, a pretty sight that would entrance
The hardest heart, one discord sometimes rent the air,
And scattered all the nervous creatures who lived there.

Echo it was, who, careless of the atmosphere
Would always chatter, shriek with laughter, argue there.
For she was charged by Zeus to keep his wife amused
With idle tales; who whilst her back was turned, abused
Her trust by taking other lovers in those glades.

When she found out this made the Queen go pale with rage.

Thus, as a punishment for what Echo had done,
Queen Hera placed enchantment on her loosened tongue.
"You always had to have the last word!" Hera said,
"And now that's ALL you'll have!"

     At these words Echo fled

Sobbing down the mountainside to foothills below,

And wandered sadly round, not knowing where to go.

Then bye and bye, she spied a handsome shepherd boy,
And fell in love at once.
     Unable to employ
Her voice to tell this paragon of her heart true,
She followed him about.
     "What can I do for you?"
He asked her curtly, with a cold indifference cruel.
"For you........for you............."
     Echo repeated, like a fool.

Index :
Green lacewing, Keeled skimmer dragonfly, Luber grasshopper, Comma butterfly, Speckled wood butterfly, Beautiful demoiselle. (m)

Since this boy, Narcissus, ...was very vain indeed,
And when the girls   .... fell for his looks he took no heed,
He spurned   .... the calf-eyed goddess who trailed after him,
And unrequited love made her grow pale and thin.
"Oh go away, you stupid girl! You're boring me!"
"Ring me.............ring me................."   repeated Echo mis'rably.

Her broken heart turned icy, and she cursed him then.
"I wish that YOU would suffer as I do, and when
You fall in love, your love will treat you as badly
As you have treated me!" she pined despondently.

Queen Hera thought about what she had done, and sent
Her maids to find Echo and tell her:~ "I repent ~"
But when they searched the rocks and wooded places, their
Voices were caught away and floated on the air.
"Echo!........Echo!" they called, which came back on the breeze,
"Echo!........Echo!" reverberating through the trees.

For she had wandered off, and faded right away......
Only her voice remained, and even to this day
When you are by the mountain, closed in valley walls,
You'll hear her voice repeating everybody's calls.........

Meanwhile Narcissus went and sat beside a mere,
And stared at his reflection in the water there.
"How beautiful!"
he cried, and tried to touch those lips,
Which made the face dissolve beneath his fingertips.
The more he tried, the worse it got, and in it's place
The ripples spoilt the perfect image of his face.
So he sat still, and gazed, until he just took root,
And where he sat, instead of boy, a new green shoot
Began to grow, and turned into a yellow flower,
Leaning out across the pond, wanting to admire
It's own reflection in the water of that pool;
So perfect, and so delicate, in shade so cool.

And to this day you'll see Narcissi growing here and there,
But shepherd-boy, like Echo, has vanished into air.

Index:
Beautiful demoiselle, Green lacewing, Keeled skimmer dragonfly,
Swallowtail, Peacock butterfly Painted lady, Speckled wood, Cabbage white, Comma butterfly

THE TWELVE LABOURS OF HERACLES
*(More usually known by the Roman version of his name
HERCULES, here we use the GREEK name HERACLES)*

The high divorce rate of our age
Can complicate our parentage
But this is nothing when compared
To gods and half-gods, who all shared
A web of strange relationships
With which it's hard to get to grips.

Take HERACLES, the strongest one;
Although he was great Zeus's son
His mother wed Amphitryon
Who went to war;
          whilst he was gone
Zeus took his place;
          then back from war
Came husband, so TWO sons she bore.
    One by the god, called HERACLES,
    And twin by husband, Iphicles.

Now Heracles was very strong -
A trait he showed from very young,
And Zeus's queen called Hera was
So jealous of this son, she caused
Two snakes to creep into his cot,
But he just tied them in a knot!

Throughout his life Queen Hera schemed
To thwart the plans of which he dreamed,
And caused him rages in which he
Would rampage on a killing spree.
So first he used his lyre to slay
The man who taught him how to play;
Went on to kill his family......................

And so was sent to slavery
In order that he might redeem
His manhood and his self esteem;
And set twelve labours so that he
Could rehabilitated be.

Index: Toe-biter beetles, aka electric light bug or giant water bug.

Authors's note: The so-called Hercules beetle was not selected for the role of Heracles because it is a vegetarian whose larval stage is a grub (which could not strangle snakes!) The male uses its large horn to fight other males.

To bear these labours all in mind
Can sometimes prove to be a bind,
So just recall this little rhyme
To try to save yourself some time.

1 First Lion's skin

2 then Hydra's head,

3 The golden hind

4 the boar so dread

5 Augean stables must be clean

6 Then shoot those birds so fierce and mean

7 Go on to capture Bull of Crete

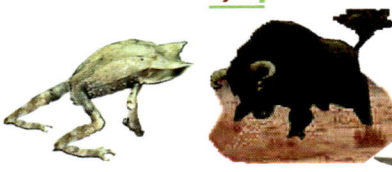

8 Make Mares of Diomedes eat
Their master, leaving them replete,

9 Take girdle from Queen Hippolyte,

10 Herd cattle of Ceryon, seize

11 The apples of Hesperides

12 And last of all he had to steal
The three-head dog that guarded hell.

*Author's note: In this rhyme Hippolyte is Hippo-leet but the correct pronounciation of Hippolyte is HIP-POLLY-TEE

15

The Nemean Lion

First, Heracles was sent to kill
The giant lion that roamed the hill.
Immune to weapons, it would scour
The land for people to devour.

Our hero found it in it's den;

He grabbed it round the throat and then
He shook it by it's massive head,
And wrung it's neck 'till it was dead.

He skinned it, and then placed the hide
Across his shoulders strong and wide,
And tied the paws in front to make
A garment for his own keepsake.

The Lernaean Hydra

You'd think the King would, as agreed,
Congratulate him on this deed;
But not a bit of it! Instead
He told him: "Now go kill the dread
Swamp-monster Hydra." (which, no doubt
The King believed would take him out!)

So Heracles set out again
And found the monster in the fen.
He slashed one head off, but it grew
In place of that, another two!
He swung his sword this way and that,
But every time, two heads grew back!

So Heracles drew back a bit -
A fiercely-burning fire he lit,
And thrust his club right into it,
Which made the end glow red and spit.

Then, taking up his trusty sword,
Right back into the fray he roared.

To left and right, with twist and turn,
With one hand slice, the other burn.
He cut the head, then seared it through,
Preventing it from growing two.

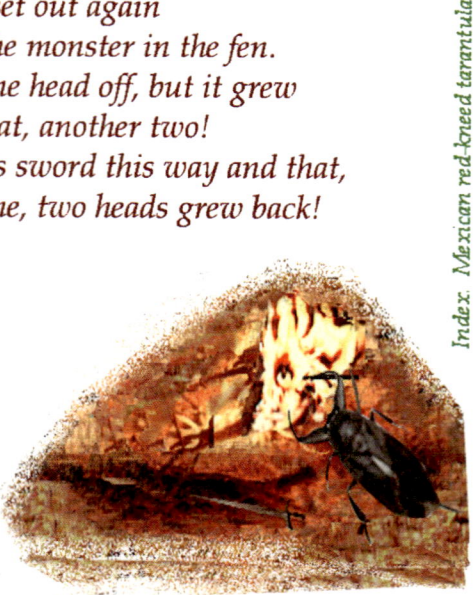

At last - reduced to just a stump -
He left a harmless twisted rump.

Index: Mexican red-kneed tarantula
Toe-biter
Round-leaved sundew (~ *Drosera rotundifolia* ~)

16

The Ceryneian Hind

Eurystheus began to rave -
"How CAN I rid me of this slave?
He's far too strong - I'll have to make
A plan as cunning as a snake.
Perhaps the gods could help me here?
I'll make him catch the sacred deer
Of Artemis, who'll punish him,
(For desecrating deer's a sin!)"

Index: Bushcricket (f)
Toebiter
Broad-bodied chaser
dragonflies (m + f)

(When Artemis was just a child
She'd come across a herd of wild
Gigantic hinds, and captured some
To pull her chariot - but one
Escaped. It was so fast it could
Out-run an arrow through the wood.)

So Heracles was sent to find
That golden-antlered, brass-hoofed hind.

The hind led him a merry chase
Through Greece and Istria and Thrace,
And every now and then a glint
Of golden antlers flashed a hint.
A year went by, it stopped, it drank,
His poisoned arrow hit it's flank,
And so the doe was rendered lame
Enab'ling Heracles to tame
Her into coming back with him.
    Then, meeting Artemis and twin
    Apollo on the way, he begged
    Forgiveness of the goddess, and
    Explained how this chase had been planned.
        The goddess said she'd let him go
        Provided he returned the doe.

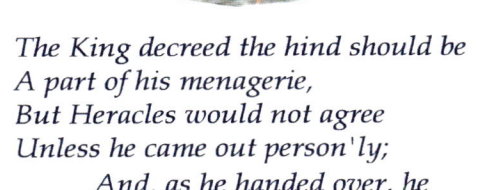

The King decreed the hind should be
A part of his menagerie,
But Heracles would not agree
Unless he came out person'ly;
    And, as he handed over, he
    Let slip the rein; ......then instantly
    The hind had
        opportunity
    To sprint back   to the goddess,
                    ....free.

Then Heracles said, "King, you know
The problem is, you're just too slow."

© Diana Knight

The Erymanthian Boar

The King was apoplectic then -
Our hero had survived AGAIN.
This upstart made him look a fool -
He MUST devise some ending cruel!
So now he schemed that our hero
To Mount Erymanthos should go...... ~ ~ ~ ~ ~ ~ ~

There was a boar that rampaged there,
And this dread creature he must snare.

Then Heracles set out to track
That fearful boar, and bring it back.

He asked the centaur Chiron for
Advice on how to catch the boar,

And Chiron told him,
"Drive it back,
And where the snow is thick,
ATTACK!"

So Heracles did as advised,
And when he caught it, he devised
A binding that enabled him
To take it back to show the King.

The King was truly PETRIFIED
When that great creature he espied.
He went and hid in a tall jar
And watched our hero from afar.

"Take it away, get RID of it!"
Eurystheus said in a fit.
~ ~ ~ ~ ~ ~ ~ ~ ~ ~ ~ ~ ~ ~ ~ ~ ~
The King, now livid, had a plan
To get his own back on our man
A most humiliating task
To tarnish him is what he'd ask.................

THE AUGEAN STABLES

"Now go and clean the stables of
The King of Elis, Augeias.
And do so in a SINGLE DAY,
But if you can't, I'll make you pay!"

Augeias had the largest herd
Of cattle, and he gave his word
To Heracles that he would pay
For cleaning stables in one day

(Augeias thought that as these kine
Had been to him a gift divine,
And could not suffer from disease,
Although in filth up to their knees
The task was just impossible
For our brave hero to fulfil.)

Index: Cockroach (Ellipsidion Australe)   Toe-biter   Wasp beetle (Clytus Arietis,

18

But Heracles confounded him
By managing this task so grim;

He dammed two rivers to rush through
The valley and clean out the goo.

Then, when he broke the dam again,
The waters rushed back whence they came.

Thus all the filth the waters bore,
To leave the stables clean once more.

Augeias had agreed to pay
One tenth of all his herd that day,

But yet, when all the work was done,
Refused to give a SINGLE ONE!

So Heracles just killed him dead,
And gave his son the land instead!

So now it once again transpired
Eurystheus's scheme back-fired.

He planned this task so Heracles
Would come home crawling on his knees

Instead of making him all bowed
It RAISED his status with the crowd!

Eurystheus began to shout -
"The WATERS washed the stables out!

That doesn't count! You're just a cheat!
You needn't think you've got me beat!

Index: Wasp beetle, Toe biter
Cardinal beetle, weevils

There's PLENTY more for you to do
Before your labouring is through!"

19

Stymphalian Birds

Now there were some man-eating birds,
With claws of brass, and toxic turds,
And sharp metalic feathers they
Could launch, to kill their chosen prey.

They came to Lake Stymphalus to
Escape a pack of wild wolves, who
Had kept their numbers down; but could
Now breed unhindered in the wood.

And, spreading out like a disease,
They soon destroyed the crops and trees.

Now Heracles was told he should
Get rid of those birds from the wood.

The forest round the lake was dark ~
He couldn't see to shoot them.

Athena and Hephaestus made
Some clappers, to uproot them.

So, with this help,
    our hero could
Flush out those birds
    from in that wood;
And, when they flew up
    in a fright,
His arrows hit them
    in mid-flight

Index : Locusts, Toe-biter

And those that did not perish then
Did not return to Greece again.

THE CRETAN BULL

Next, Heracles was told to sail
To Crete, to catch the Cretan Bull.
(The King thought that it would suffice
As an important sacrifice.)

Now Minos, King of Crete, was glad
To have that bull caught, as it had
Been wrecking havoc all about
And really should be taken out.

You see, in Crete the bulls were sought
By brave young men, to use for sport.
They used to run up and accost
The bull by both the horns, which tossed
Those fearless men into the air;

They somersaulted out of there,

And, flying right across it's hide,
They landed safe on t'other side.

But THIS bull didn't go to plan,
And here is how it all began:

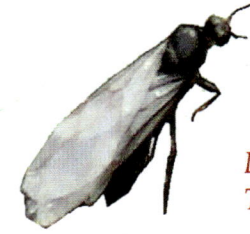

When Minos, as he claimed the throne,
Had tried to prove that he alone
Deserved the right to be the King,
The ruler over everything,

He undertook a solemn vow;
He told the god Poseidon how
Whatever he sent from the sea
A sacrifice to him would be.

Poseidon sent a handsome bull -
But it was just SOoooooooooo beautiful
That Minos went and lost his head,
And killed another bull instead.

This made the sea-god foam and rage -
He sent his bull on a rampage,
And made the wife of Minos fall
In love with that great beast, withall!

So as a consequence she bore
That hybrid called the Minotaur.

(With limbs of man and head of bull
This was a beast so terrible
That people fled in awe and fear
If ever they should get too near.
So Minos built a maze beneath
His palace for the monster's keep.)

Bold Heracles sought out the bull,
And choked it until it was still.

Then, having bound it tightly, he
Arranged to ship it home by sea.

But,
having proved he'd passed the test,
Eurystheus was not impressed...
"The bull's not fit for purpose!" he
Decided, inconsistently.

(For Hera, who he had in mind
To sacrifice it to, declined
To find the gift acceptable,
'Cos Heracles had caught the bull.

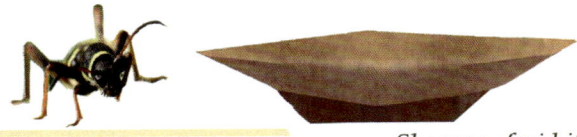

She was afraid it would be HE
Who got the glory, 'stead of she,
And so the bull could not appease,
Because she hated Heracles.)

The King released it, whereupon
It wandered into Marathon,
And terrified the populace
By rampaging about the place,

'Till Theseus had come along
And killed the bull. (He then went on
To kill the Minotaur as well,
A tale that we will later tell.)

Index: Malaysian horned toad (Megophrys montana)
Wood ants; Thorny devil (Molach horridus)

21

THE MARES OF DIOMEDES

So of his labours to this date
Our hero stands at number eight.

Next Heracles was sent to bring
Some wild horses to the king.

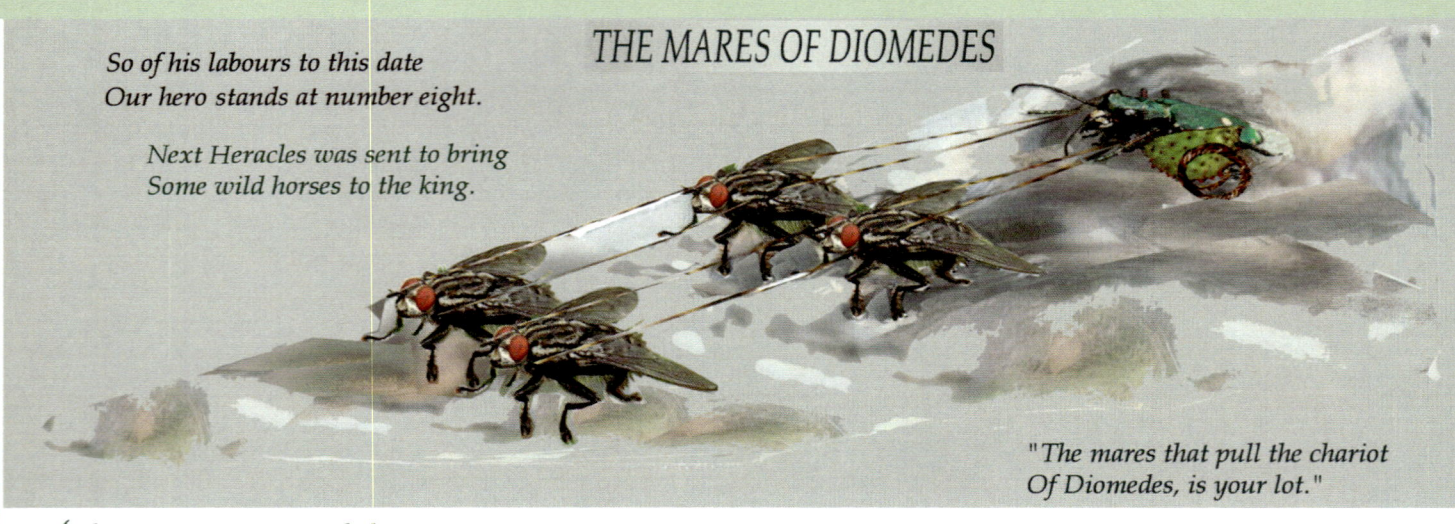

"The mares that pull the chariot
Of Diomedes, is your lot."

(The Bristones were a tribal race
Who lived beside the sea in Thrace.
              Diomedes, their giant king,
              Ruled fiercely over everything)

So Heracles went with all speed
To those bronze stables where these steed
Were kept in chains;
           but did not know
The reason why this should be so.

(Eurystheus did not confess ~
These mares were fed on human flesh)

He left a youth called Abderos
To guard the mares, whilst he went off
To fight Diomedes; but when
            He brought that giant back again
            He found the mares had killed the youth
            And eaten him; ~ so now the truth
                  Of those four mares' strange appetite
                  By accident was brought to light.

And so he killed Diomedes
And fed him to his own cruel steed.

This calmed the horses; so he bound
Their mouths shut, and went on to found
The city called Abdera, near
The tomb of that poor youth so dear.

On his return Eurystheus
Decided that a gift to Zeus
Would be a good idea, and so
To Mount Olympus he must go.

But Zeus would not accept the mares,
And lions, wolves and wild bears
Were sent to savage them; a just
                And fitting end to their blood-lust.

Index: Green Tiger beetle (Cicindela campestris)
           Flesh flies (Sarcophaga Carnaria)
           Toebiters

HIPPOLYTE'S BELT

Next, Heracles was sent by sea,
To meet with Queen Hip~poly~te,
The ruler of the Amazons,
A warrior tribe, who cast out sons,
But raised their daughters to be skilled
At waging war without being killed.

And to this end, so they could throw
A lance with ease, or draw a bow,
They each cut off their right-side breast,
So that at fighting they'd be best.

The art of war Hippolyte
Had learned whilst at her father's knee
For he was Ares, god of war;
And round her waist she always wore
A leather girdle, which had been
A gift from him, and had unseen
Enchanted properties, which gave
It's wearer strength, and made her brave.  
She kept her weapons in this band,
To have both sword and spear to hand.

Eurystheus desired this belt
To give HIS daughter, 'cos he felt
It would enhance her status; ……… so ……… ……
Commanded Heracles to go
And get it, by foul means or fair,
And then to bring it back from there.

Now Heracles would not survive
Alone against that fearsome tribe
Of women-warriors, and so
His friends had all agreed to go
And fight with him; so with that crew
His ship came sailing into view.

The Queen, who saw them out at sea,
Came down to greet them at the quay,
And she agreed to his request
To take the girdle from her chest.

Index: Hornet (vespa crabro), Toe-biter, wasp beetle

23

But Hera had been watching, and
She had another idea planned,
Because she hated Heracles,
And couldn't bear to see him pleased.

So, putting all her armour on,
She dressed-up like an Amazon,
And spread a rumour round that he
Planned to ABDUCT Hippolyte.

So ALL the Amazons put on
Their armour, and they rushed on down
Towards the sea, to save their queen;

But this approaching horde was seen;

Believing that it must be she
Who had betrayed them heartlessly,
Now Heracles quick-thinkingly
Attacked and killed Hippolyte,

Then grabbed the girdle from her waist,
And, turning back to sea, he raced
Aboard his ship, and sailed away.

Index: Keeled skimmer dragonfly, European hornets, Toe-biter

So lived to fight another day.

24

THE CATTLE OF GERYON

There was a monster ~ GERYON ~
Most horrible to look upon.
Three heads, twelve limbs, on bodies three,
He was a frightful sight to see.
He lived on Erytheia, and
Had sentinels to guard his land.

Because he owned some special kine ~
A type of cattle most divine.

Index: Wolf spider (with three heads)
Seed bug (Lygaeus saxatlis)

The King now set a tenth task grim ~
To steal those oxen back to him,
So he could sacrifice them to
The goddess Hera, (as you do........)
Which meant our hero had to fell
That monster, and the guards as well.
Then single-handedly survive
The hardship of the cattle drive.

As he set out to do this feat
That desert, in the searing heat
Beat on his back, and burned his feet,
'Till he was tempted to retreat;
And in a fit of temper, shot
An arrow at that sun so hot.
This caused Apollo to implore
That he desist, and shoot no more.

Our hero said he would comply
If he could travel 'cross the sky
Just like the sun-god did, inside
His golden orb at eventide.

The bargain struck, the arrows ceased;
He hitched a ride from west to east
Across the ocean, to that isle
Whereon there lived that monster vile.

Now Orthrus, two-head guardian
(And brother to the hound of hell
Called Cerberus) was waiting for
Our hero as he stepped ashore.

    A fierce battle then ensued;
    Our hero used his method crude ~
    He raised his club, then brought it down
    To split both heads from nape to crown.

    Eurytion, the herdsman, heard
    The noise of battle, and appeared
    To help his fellow guardian;
    But Heracles just struck him down.

    Then Geryon sprang into play,
    And scuttled down to join the fray.

He wore 3 helmets on his heads,
3 pairs of greaves encased his legs,
Each pair of arms had spear and shield;
The sight alone would make men yield.

    But Heracles was not deterred
    (To danger he was quite immured)
    A poisoned arrow from his bow
    Went flying fast towards his foe

    And struck him in the head, which bent
    His neck, and from his body rent
    A shrill despairing cry; he swayed;
    He tottered groaning, all dismayed;
    Then fell down dead, ne'er more to rise ~

    Now Heracles could claim his prize.

*The journey home was hard and long
As everything kept going wrong;
For Hera, all along the way
Provoked the cows to go astray;*

    *Which gave our hero lots of grief,
    And nearly made him fail his brief.
    But finally the herd was brought
    Back to Eurystheus's court.*

    The King then sacrificed them to
    Ungrateful goddess Hera, who
    Had made our hero's task so grim,
    Because she'd always hated him.

Index: Centipede (with 2 heads); Toe biter; Jewel beetle; Wolf spider (with 3 heads and armour); Seed bugs; Wasp beetle.

The Garden of Hesperides

The garden if Hesperides
Was planted with enchanted trees,
Grown from the fruited branches which
Had been Earth-goddess Gaia's gift
To Zeus and Hera, when they wed.
It's golden fruit immortals fed.

And Hera sent the daughters of
Great Atlas (who held up the sky)
And Herperis (the evening star)
To guard her apples, and de-bar
Those seekers of her treasure-trove
Who might try stealing from her grove.

A many-headed dragon*
  kept
A watchful eye, in case
  they slept,
Or, careless of their
  duties, strayed
Or ate the fruit
  themselves,
    or slept.

Now Heracles was sent to bring
Those magic apples to his King.

So, seeing Atlas
by and by,
He asked him to
put down the sky,

And fetch the apples
  in his stead.
"I'll hold the sky for you," he said.
(For truth to tell, he feared to fight
'Gainst many-headed Ladon's might)

The Titan granted this request ~
It WOULD be nice to take a rest!
He got the fruit with ease, and then
RELUCTANTLY returned again.

The thought of taking back the sky
Was 'nough to make a TITAN cry!
And so he said to Heracles
"YOU stay, and I'LL deliver these!"

But Heracles was much too bright
To let that Titan out of sight.
He just PRETENDED he'd agreed,
But asked if he could be relieved,
So he could place his lion's skin
About his back, for cushioning.
Then soon as Atlas took the sky ~
He grabbed the fruit, and said GOODBYE!

Index: Sisters: The common wasp
  (vespula vulgaris)
Dragon: A nest of slow worms.
Heracles : A toe-biter
Atlas : A hanging fly.

Author's note: The name of the dragon was Ladon.* In this story there are usually 3 sisters, although sometimes 4 or up to 7.

CERBERUS

Author's warning: change in meter

The last task of Heracles,
Which should bring him to his knees:~
To capture the three-head dog
That guarded the gate
Which led to the Underworld;
No live man should enter there,
Whilst dead men for evermore
To stay, was their fate.

Preparing himself for this
He first went to Eleusis,
To learn all the mysteries
Surrounding this case....
With help of Athena and
Winged Hermes the messenger
He had to get in~and~out
Of that morbid place.

Index:
Heracles: A toebiter
Cerebus: A three-headed centipede (Haplophilus Subterraneus)
Hermes: A dragonfly
Charon: A pond skater
Dead souls: Bombadier beetles

When dead souls first enter there
They come to the River Styx,
And then have to get across
To the other side.
And Charon, the ferryman,
Will take them across if they
Have with them an obolus,
To pay for the ride.

So now Heracles set forth
To enter the Underworld,
And Hermes assisted him
In this enterprise.
And Charon the ferryman
Allowed him to pass because
He pulled such a fearsome face,
And screwed up his eyes.

28

Remember we saw before ~
The King who resided here
Had taken Persephone
To be his fair bride.

As Zeus was her father, she
Was sister to Heracles,
And so he was confident
She'd be on his side.

Then Heracles stood before
Their throne, and entreated them
To let him take out that hound
With howling mouths wide.

And they answered "Very well" ~
Provided no harm befell
Their guard dog resulting from
It's visit outside.

And so he must master it
Without use of weapons which
Might damage in any way
That dangerous hound.

Then Heracles wrestled it,
And dragged it until it slid
Protesting and slavering
Up from underground.

Where spittle from Cerberus
Fell on to the ground above
There sprang from
corrupted earth
~In those hissing spots~
The first deadly poison plants
Including the aconite
Which thenceforth the
Grecians used
In murderous plots.

When he saw fierce Cerberus
That coward Eurystheus
Afraid of that fearsome beast
Hid in the large urn.

Thus having completed all
His tasks for Eurystheus
Brave Heracles kept his word
The dog to return.

29

HICKORY D'ICARUS

An ant's a social creature,
*   as you and I both know.*
If you're an ant you have to go
*   where all the others go.*

You're born into a system
    with one unbroken rule -
You know your place,
    you tow the line,
        you never play the fool.

An ant heap is a city,
    a queen lives at it's heart,
And all her subjects know their role,
    and gamely play their part.

Attendants groom and feed her,
    while she produces strings
Of pearly eggs, which midwives carry off to nursery wings.

The eggs are piled in batches, to keep them safe and snug -
For there are lots of insects who would eat a tasty grub!

The adults guard and feed them, and check the thermostat -
An egg must have good air-conditioning, no doubt of that!

It grows until it hatches, then nanny ants advise it
On all the skills a little ant will need to socialise it.

And so it reaches adulthood inexorably fated
To carry out the purposes for which it's mater mated.

Thus some will guard, and some will tend, and some will fetch and carry,
And some will grow transparent wings, and leave the nest, and marry.

Then males die off, and new young queens will make it their vocation
To hibernate through winter in a suitable location.

So come the spring, when she revives, the new queen in ascendance
Will build a nest, and her first eggs will hatch into attendants.

And so the cycle starts again, it really is relentless,
A boring rhythm giving rise to lives that are eventless.

Index: Middle : Meadow ant with cocoon:
       Centre : Large wood ant with tiny wood ant
       Bottom: Meadow ants with wings.

EXCEPT........................

© Diana Knight 2007

In old tale ridicalous
A young ant called Icarus
Who's wings wouldn't stick-arus
Fell into the sea.
His father was Daedalus,
Who was locked inside-alous
Which made him decide-alous
"This fate's not for me."

For he was the architect
Of fabulous labyrinth
Which ran underneath the heap
By royal decree.
But when he had finished it
He wasn't allowed to leave
For fear he would spread the word
Of how to break free.

When he made the labyrinth
He was very proud of it,
But then he found out that it
Was used as a trap.
A monster who lived in it
Who was called the Minotaur
Ate ants who were lost in it
Without a good map.

Now though he was not the sort
To have wings, Daedalus thought
He'd copy the ones he saw
On those who flew by.
So he stuck together bits
Of gossamer feather-bits
All strapped on with leather-bits
To take to the sky.

And he told young Icarus
To his side to stick-arus,
And not to fly up into
The heat of the sun.
"Those hot rays are dangerous
So stay within range-erous
Or your wings will change-erous
And down you will come."

But when they jumped off into
The wide sky so free and blue
Young Icarus thought that this
Was really good fun.
And so he just soared on high
Ignoring the heartfelt cry
"Get back or your wings will fry!
Oh what have you done!"

So Icarus came unstuck
Because he had run amok
Ignoring the good advice
Which Daedalus gave.
And as he went plunging down
His whole world was spinning round
And he struck the sea to drown
In watery grave.

Author's note:
Readers who recognise that the relationship between two worker wood ants could not be father/son should substitute the word 'sister' for 'father,' and 'she' for 'he'. Whilst this will make the story correct entomologically (since wingless ants are both infertile and female) it will render it incorrect mythologically.

KING MIDAS

Once there was a foolish king called Midas,
Whose silly antics really would have tried us.
His favourite friend was Pan, who played the pipes,
(Such merry-making is what Midas likes)

A music competition on the 'morrow
To see who played the best, Pan or Apollo,
Had been pre-judged by Midas, who ignored
The merits of the play for this award.

Although Apollo knew HE was the best,
Midas INSISTED that he'd FAILED the test.
"If that is what you think," Apollo sneers,
"Then there is something wrong with your poor ears!"

"My ears are fine!" says Midas haughtily -
"Oh really?" says Apollo naughtily.
He cast a spell on Midas' ears, which twitched
And grew into long ass's ears, bewitched.

Index: Emperor moth (m), Hoverfly (m), Broad-bodied chaser dragonfly (m)

King Midas was appalled, and wore a hat -
He knew his ass's ears would be laughed at!
But when he saw his barber for a trim
He HAD to let her see his ears so grim.

"You must tell NO-ONE of this defect dire!"
    "Your secret's safe with me, oh royal sire!"
But though the barber tried to do her best
She laughed so VERY much it hurt her chest.

It really was a trial to keep it down,
So one day she just walked right out of town,

And dug a hole, and stuck her head inside;
"KING MIDAS HAS LONG ASS'S EARS!" she cried.

Author's note: Of course in the original story the barber was a 'he', but for the sake of the entomologists amoungst my readers I have had to change this to a 'she' because the illustration is of a female praying mantis.

Meanwhile our king had come across a faun
Who'd lost his way, and hungry and forlorn
Was grateful when he got a breakfast dish,
And for that favour said he'd grant a wish.

Longhorn beetle (m) with Midas (Emperor moth)

King Midas SHOULD have wished away his curse,
Instead of which he thought about his purse.
"Grant all I touch will turn to solid gold!"
Which was not wise, but he would not be told.

"If you insist!" the satyr said, "but THINK!
When all is gold you cannot eat or drink!"
That silly fat-head had condemned himself
In such a greedy bid for boundless wealth.

His servants turned to gold, so did his son.
"Oh NO!" moaned Midas, "Look what I have done!"
"I told you so!" the faun popped in to say -
"I TOLD you you would live to rue the day!

But you insisted, against all the odds!"
"Please take it back!" begged Midas, "Ask the gods
To lift it off!" ---The satyr did his stuff ---
"With EARS LIKE THAT
        I think you've woes enough!

"Just go and dip yourself into the river" -
This Midas did,
        which proved a true life-giver,
And thus restored, that foolish king made bold
To wash his golden palace free of gold.

Index: Top: Longhorn beetle (m) with Midas (Emperor moth)
Middle: Longhorn, leaf bug. Emperor moth caterpillar, Stag beetle (m), Midas

34

ORPHEUS & EURYDICE
A Madrigal Song

Let's tell a sad love story
Of souls in purgatory.......
(With a heartfelt sympathy we sing,
With a heartfelt sympathy)
Of Orpheus and wife,
The light of his whole life......
(With a heartfelt sympathy we sing,
With a heartfelt sympathy)

One day when he was playing
~ For he was a musician ~
(With a trembling chord upon his lyre,
With a chord upon his lyre)
And oh! how he could play!
He'd melt your heart away!
(With a trembling chord upon his lyre,
With a chord upon his lyre)

Eurydice, his dear one
Cried out, and then she fell down ~
(With a heartfelt sympathy we sing,
With a heartfelt sympathy)
He caught her in his arms
His heart beat with alarms
(With a heartfelt sympathy we sing,
With a heartfelt sympathy)

"My darling! What's the matter?"
Alas! she could not answer;
(With a why, oh why is she so pale?
With a why is she so pale?)
She'd slipped her mortal coil
A snake bite told the tale
(With the mark of fangs upon her heel,
With the poison in her heel)

"I cannot live without her!
I'll have to go and get her!"
(With a heartfelt sympathy we sing,
With a heartfelt sympathy)
"Down to the world below ~
That's where I will now go!"
(With a 'No live man can enter there'
With a 'There you cannot go')

His friends all gasped with horror
At such a bold idea
(With a 'Don't be foolish, you can't go'
With a 'There you cannot go')
But he was not deterred:
He was good as his word;
(With a 'I will go and fetch her back'
With a 'I will get her back')

Index : Cicada, dark Plant-hopper, (ghost) green Plant-hopper, (audience) Comma and Brimstone butterflies, Devil's coach-horse beetle, Prelate beetle, flower fly, 2 cockroaches

He travelled to that river
Which dead souls must cross over
    (With a fa-la, la-la, la la la,
    With a fa-la, la-la, la)
And called out "Ferryman!
Come take me over yon!"
    (With a gentle drip and splash of oars,
    With a gentle splash of oars)

"Dear sir, you must be crazy,
None but the dead may cross here!"
    (With a gentle drip and splash of oars,
    With a gentle splash of oars)
"And even if I did,
You cannot pass the guard"
    (With a gentle drip and splash of oars,
    With a gentle splash of oars)

"Please just do as I say, man,
And love will find a way, man!"
    (With a gentle drip and splash of oars,
    With a gentle splash of oars)
Then Charon's heart did melt,
The young man's grief he felt,
    (With a fa-la, la-la, la la la,
    With a fa-la, la-la, la)

And so he rowed him over
To rescue his true lover
    (With a gentle drip and splash of oars,
    With a gentle splash of oars)
And as they glided in
They heard a frightful din
    (With a fa-la, la-la, la la la,
    With a fa-la, la-la, la)

"That's Cerberus, the guardian,
I told you you can't pass him"
    (With a gentle drip and splash of oars,
    With a gentle splash of oars)
But Orpheus just took
His lyre with artful look,
    (With a fa-la. la-la, la la la,
    With a fa-la, la-la, la)

His fingers weaved their magic,
And filled that place so tragic
    (With a softly soothing harmony,
    With a soothing harmony)
With melodies divine:
The barks became a whine
    (When Cerebus heard that soothing sound,
    When he heard that soothing sound)

Then dead souls stopped to listen
And Cerberus, the guardian
 (When he heard that soothing harmony,
 When he heard that harmony)
 Laid down his heads and slept
 And over him they stepped.
 (With a fa-la, la-la, la la la,
  With a fa-la, la-la, la)

When Hades, in his palace,
Heard that forbidden music
        (What softly soothing harmony,
         What a soothing harmony)
He asked Persephone
"Whatever can that be?"
     (With a softly soothing harmony,
      With a soothing harmony)

"That's Orpheus, musician
Who plays with such emotion!"
        (With a fa-la, la-la, la la la,
         With a fa-la, la-la, la)
"With such a melody
It can be none but he!"
     (With a softly soothing harmony,
      With a soothing harmony)
"If he is dead, his spirit
Will give us better music
     (With a softly soothing harmony,
      With a soothing harmony)
"Down here than up above!
Let it be so, my love!"
     (With a fa-la, la-la, la la la,
      With a fa-la, la-la, la)

"There is no music down here,
 As you well know my own dear!"
     (With a fa-la, la-la, la la la,
      With a fa-la, la-la, la)

Then Orpheus appeared,
In mortal body clothed!
    (What a shocking sight to see in there!
     What a shocking sight to see!)
Then Hades shouted; "Young man!
I'll make you rue this rash plan!"
    (What a shocking sight to see in there!
     What a shocking sight to see!)
But Orpheus, unmoved
Just sang about his love.
     (With a softly soothing harmony,
      With a soothing harmony)

37

He sang of her great beauty;
He sang of love and duty:
(With a voice so sweet and low he sang,
With a voice so sweet and low)
Of bite of spiteful snake:
Of terrible heartache:
(With a voice so sweet and low he sang,
With a voice so sweet and low)

Then Hades fell back weeping,
Said with a gesture sweeping
(For the song had pierced him to the heart,
It had pierced him to the heart)
"Many folk have pleaded
None of them I've heeded"
(For the song had pierced him to the heart,
It had pierced him to the heart)

"But I cannot say no, so
Eurydice may now go............"
(For the song had pierced him to the heart,
It had pierced him to the heart)
"But you must not turn round
'Till you're above the ground"
(For the song had pierced him to the heart,
It had pierced him to the heart)

Orpheus was reassured:
Hades would keep to his word
(With a light footfall that followed him
A light footfall followed him)
And so he turned his back
To leave that pit so black
(With a light footfall which followed him
A light footfall followed him)

Throughout that gruesome journey
He longed to turn round and see~
(But the light footfall still followed him,
Yes, it always followed him)
But, looking straight ahead,
He played his lyre instead
(And the light footfall still followed him,
Yes, it always followed him)

When he reached the River Styx,
Eyes on t'other side were fixed,
(But the light footfall still followed him,
Yes, it always followed him)
Then Cerberus, beguiled,
Lolled like a docile child,
(And the light footfall still followed him,
Yes, it always followed him)

He came back to the long boat
Which rowed across that
           wide moat
  (With a light footfall that followed him,
    A light footfall followed him)

And when he climbed inside
He heard her hitch a ride
  (With a light footfall she stepped inside,
    A light footfall stepped inside)

Then the boat began to glide
As they reached the other side;
  (With a fa-la, la-la, la-la la,
    With a fa-la, la-la la)

He stepped ashore and climbed,
He hoped she was behind,
  (Could he hear her footsteps following?
    Did her footsteps follow him?)

When he saw the light ahead,
He was seized with sudden dread
  (Did a light footfall still follow him?
    Did her footsteps follow him?)

He just had to be sure
That she was really there,
  (Could he hear her footsteps following?
    Did her footsteps follow him?)

He glanced over his shoulder,
He wanted to behold her
  (With a nearly there, so nearly there,
    With a nearly, nearly there)

He saw her lovely face,
Her arms stretched to embrace
  (With a nearly there, so nearly there,
    With a nearly, nearly there)

Her mouth stretched in an 'O', she
Entreated him "Don't leave me!"
  (With a nearly there, so nearly there,
    With a nearly, nearly there)

But much to his dismay
She faded right away
  (With a nearly there, so nearly there,
    With a nearly, nearly there)

Then he fell down to his knees,
And he cried
          "NO! Don't go, PLEASE!
  (With a why, oh why did you turn round?
    With a why did you turn round?)

Alas! It was too late,
His glance had sealed her fate,
  (With a why, oh why did you turn round?
    With a why did you turn round?)

Orpheus was in despair,
And he howled and pulled his hair.
   (With a bitter cry, a tearful sigh,
   With a bitter, bitter cry)
And though his life went on,
His raison d'etre was gone
   (With a woe is me, oh misery,
   With a woe is, woe is me)

When he got back home again
All his playing showed his pain,
   (With a mournful tune, a tearful tone,
   With a mournful, mournful tune)
His broken heart still pined
For true love left behind,
   (With a mournful tune, a sobbing sound,
   With a mournful, mournful tune)

Then his audience grew mad
And asked "MUST you be so sad?"
   (With a dreary tune, a weary tune,
   With a dreary, weary tune)
In time their patience snapped,
And the player was attacked
   (With a sobbing sound, a tearful tone,
   With a mournful, mournful tune)

Then his spirit was released,
And he gladly welcomed death,
   (With a fa-la, la-la, la la la.
   With a fa-la, la-la la)
He thought "At last! I'll be
With my Eurydice!"
   (With a fa-la, la-la, la la la,
   With a fa-la, la-la la)

But because his music had
Made the gods so glad ~ and sad ~
   (With the skilful way his fingers play,
   With the artful, skilful way)
They could not let him go
To that dark place below
   (With a fa-la, la-la, la la la,
   With a fa-la, la-la la)

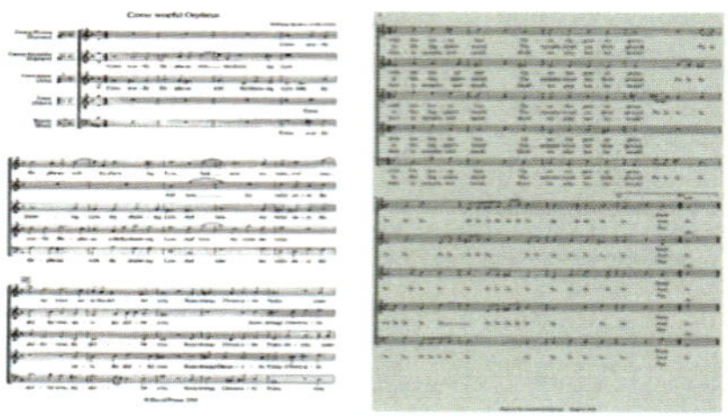

So his lyre was turned to stars
Where it's presence still inspires,
   (With eternal music of the years,
   With the music of the spheres)
Now two spirits set free
Float in true harmony,
   (With never parted more shall be,
   Throughout all eternity)

Index: Tree-hopper, Cicada (audience)Comma & Brimstone butterflies,2 Cockroaches, Devil's coach-horse beetle, Fregate beetle (attackers) Spider-hunting wasp, Fregate beetle, Robber-fly, Toe-biter, Flower-fly

PANDORA'S BOX

It's time to say "Hi"
To the useful fruit fly.
Who has opened the locks
To Pandora's strong box
And extracted the plan
For the genome of man.

Researching physicians
And skillful technicians
With hungry ambitions
Produce the conditions
To study the juices
A fruit fly produces.
They dry them, and freeze them,
And thoroughly squeeze them,
And smash them, and sieve them,
To find out what gives them
Genetic instruction
About their construction.

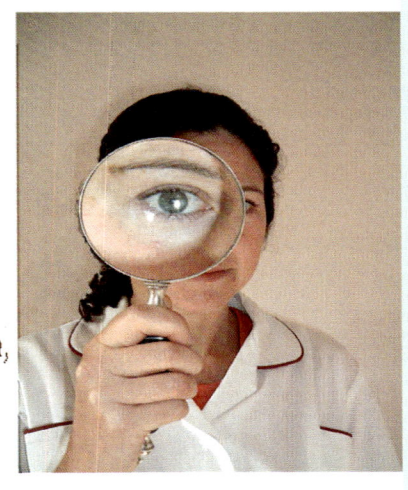

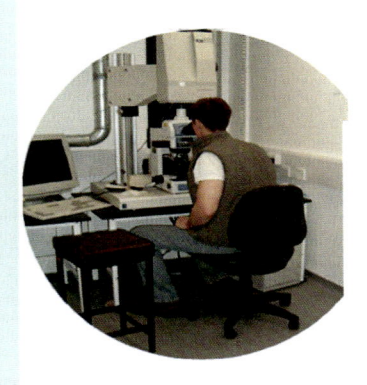

Now life's basic mystery
Revealed for all-to-see
Escapes the la-bora-t'ry
From Pandora's box.
That urge cur-i-osity
Rewards man's pre-cosity
And leads him re-lentlessly
To those building blocks.

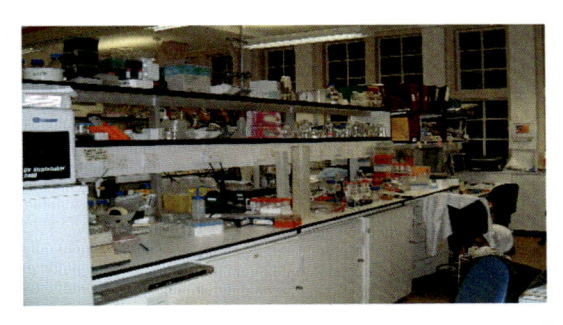

The template of earthly life
Which Adam and Eve-his-wife
Laid down for their progeny
Is written in genes.
And once we have got-the-key
We'll just have to hope-that-we
Will not make a mockery
Of all that this means.

Our tenplate will not reveal
How attributes temporal
Incorporate mystical
And all of that stuff.

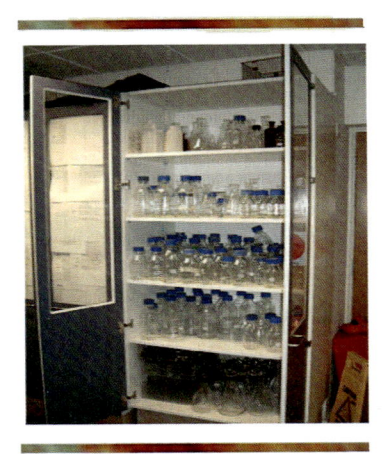

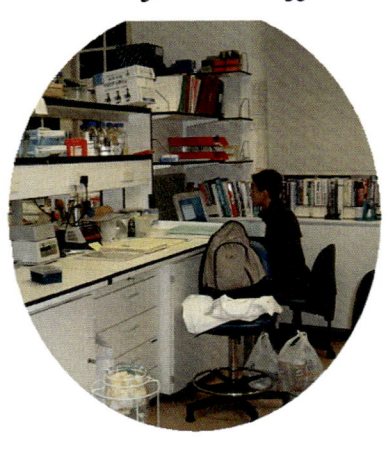

So now let's remind ourselves
Of ancient mythology
Which tells of what happens when
The going gets tough.

41

In story original
Pandora was beautiful
And skilful and dutiful
A gift from the gods.
Hephaestus was told by Zeus
To make her for man because
The cunning Prometheus
Had stolen his fire.

And then Epimetheus
   Ignoring the counsel of
   His brother Prometheus
   Took her for his wife.
Zeus fashioned a padlocked box
   And told Epimetheus
   That he mustn't open it
   For fear of his life.

And so Epimetheus
Was happy and prosperous
And told his belovèd wife
To leave it alone.
But she was too curious
And opened the box because
She couldn't resist the urge
To see what's inside.

All the human woes were there
From jealous pique, to deep despair,
And, as they hung there in the air
The stench of fear was
              everywhere.

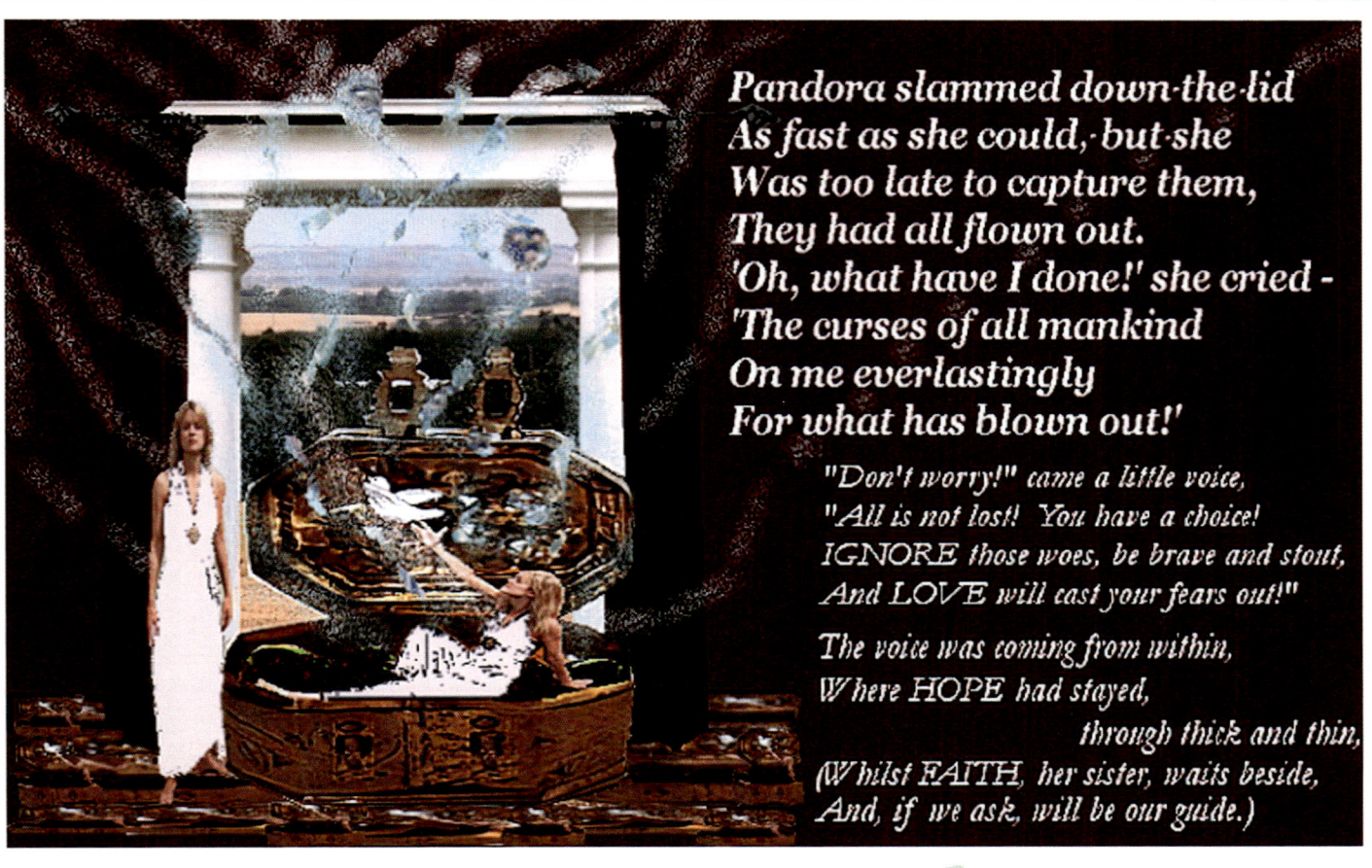

Pandora slammed down the lid
As fast as she could, but she
Was too late to capture them,
They had all flown out.
'Oh, what have I done!' she cried –
'The curses of all mankind
On me everlastingly
For what has blown out!'

"Don't worry!" came a little voice,
"All is not lost! You have a choice!
IGNORE those woes, be brave and stout,
And LOVE will cast your fears out!"

The voice was coming from within,
Where HOPE had stayed,
                      through thick and thin,
(Whilst FAITH, her sister, waits beside,
And, if we ask, will be our guide.)

Pandora opened up the box 
   And Hope 
       flew first to those harsh rocks
Where Zeus had chained Prometheus
   To punish him for stealing fire.

Prometheus felt Hope's soft breath
   And COURAGE
        flooded through his chest –
"One day some HERO will chance by
And LOOSE these chains!"
      they heard him cry.

Author's note: In other versions of this myth Pandora brings the box with her, rather than Zeus giving it to Epimetheus as a wedding gift.

And now man struggles to be free
O'er life and death gain mastery,
But should we tread more warily
Into a future we can't see?

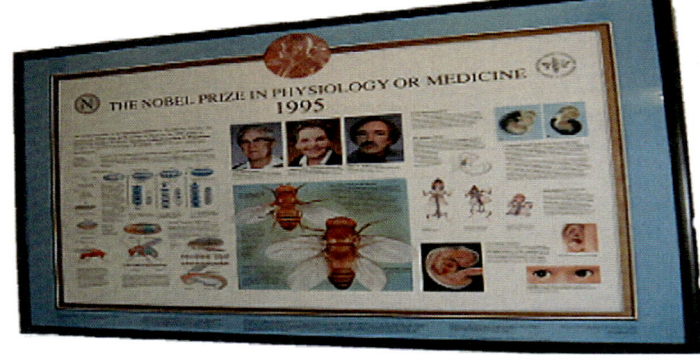

For though we have the chemistry
For reproducing you and me
The quality of charity
Is not a solid entity.

And will we leave it in or out?
And isn't that what life's about?
We NEED that magic hand unseen
That rainbows blueprint into green

The earth goddess Gaia

So............
thanks and
goodbye
To our friend
the fruit fly..
We'll catch him later   To gather more data.

Now I'm worried about Prometheus, aren't you?
And I wonder if his dream of rescue came true
Well it did - thank Zeus for that!
But first things first - let us re-cap

PROMETHEUS

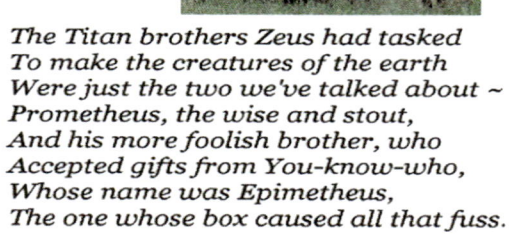

The Titan brothers Zeus had tasked
To make the creatures of the earth
Were just the two we've talked about ~
Prometheus, the wise and stout,
And his more foolish brother, who
Accepted gifts from You-know-who,
Whose name was Epimetheus,
The one whose box caused all that fuss.

This brother had the lesser art,
And so he took the humbler part ~
Prometheus watched over him
(Because, let's face it, he was dim)
Whilst he himself was set the task
Of making mankind out of mud.

So whilst his brother made those who
You might encounter in a zoo
Prometheus nursed in his breast
Ambition to turn out the best.

44

Prometheus worked skillfully,
(He was the best of potters)
   His brother gave HIS creatures gifts ~
   Some fur, some tusks, some trotters,
   A tail, a trunk, some claws, a horn,
   Some whiskers or antennae ~
   We really can't go through them ALL
   Because there were so many!

~ ~ ~ ~ ~ ~ ~ ~ ~ ~ ~ ~ ~ ~ ~ ~ ~
So by the time Prometheus
Had made HIS god-like creatures,
No gifts were left for his mud-men,
For all their god-like features!

   Prometheus felt sad about
   This lack of gifts so handy,
   And so conceived a risky plan
   To make all fine and dandy.

He waited for great Zeus to be
Engaged, and inattentive,
Then dashed up to the sun's brim to
Effect his plan
   inventive.

He stole a little stick of fire,
And hid it in a grass-stem,
Then
   gave it to his mud-men (though
      He knew it was forbidden)

   But when his mud-men USED the fire
   The SMOKE could not be hidden,
   So Zeus on Mount Olympus knew
   What gift they had been given.

~ ~
And so he charged Hephystus with the work
To make Pandora, and he took aside
The unsuspecting Epimetheus,
Who took those wondrous gifts of
                                 box and bride.

   So thus it was that all the woes escaped,
   And poor Prometheus was on the rack,
   An eagle pecked his liver out each day,
   Which, as he was a god, by night grew back.

But in his heart Zeus knew Prometheus
Did not deserve this punishment so dire ~
He LIKED those mud-men so ingenious,
Who worshipped him with altars made of fire.

   So he allowed the hero HERACLES
   To shoot the eagle that gored him each day,
   And break the chains that held him on the rock ~
   So freed, Prometheus went on his way...........

       So now we can rest easy and move on,
       For there are other things to ponder on.......

45

The trouble with a PROPHESY
Is that it sometimes comes to be
The thing that CAUSES the result,
And not the other way about.

PERSEUS

A case in point is PERSEUS,
Whose grandfather had had a curse
Predicted by the ORACLE,
Who said his daughter's son would kill
His grandfather, which made him fear
To have his daughter DANAE near.

He locked her in a tower of brass,
And guarded it, so none could pass:
But ZEUS could not be kept at bay:~
He ravished Danae anyway.
And so it wasn't Danae's fault
A son by Zeus was the result.

Then King ACRISSUS went quite mad,
And, though it made him very sad,
He went and got a wooden case,
And told his servants they must place
His daughter and her son inside,
And cast it out upon the tide.
~~~~~~~~~~~~~~~~~~~
Then, satisfied that this would serve
To solve the problem and observe
The stricture that he must not kill ~
~(For he had left them living still)~
He turned his mind to things of state
And thought that he had cheated fate.

Index: Flower fly, grasshopper, spider-hunting wasp,
Painted lady butterfly.

Meanwhile, his daughter Danae and
Her little son fetched up near land,
For, being made of wood, the box
Had floated on the sea, it's locks
Preventing their escape, but yet
Protecting them from getting wet.

A fisherman called Dictys caught
Them in his net, and gently brought
Them in to land, then set them free.
"You're welcome to come home with me,"
He said to Danae, gallantly.

Now Dictys was a good man, but
His brother ~ who was King ~ was not;
And when he first saw Danae he
Decided "I'll have HER for ME!"
(King Polydectes was his name,
Collecting wives his favourite game)

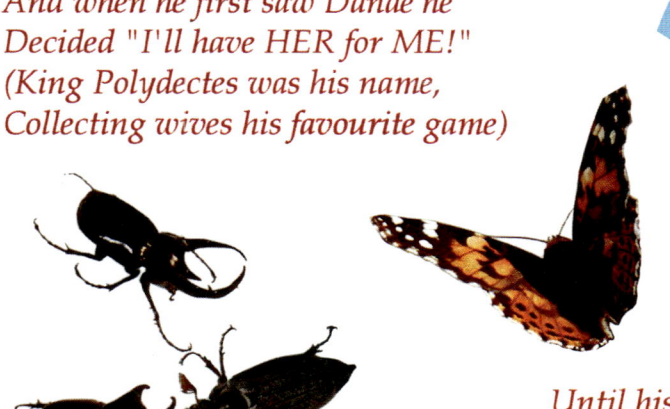

But when he asked her, she said "No!"
For years and YEARS kept saying so,
Until his patience snapped at last;
He sent his men to bind her fast
And bring her back to him, but found
That she had means to stand her ground;
For Perseus, her little son,
Had grown into a fine strong man,
Who beat those guards, and sent them home,
To tell the King: "Leave her alone!"

The King was hopping mad at this,
And ground his teeth, and clenched his fists.
"I really must dream up a ploy
To RID me of this wretched boy!"

He sent his servants back to say
Young Perseus could have his way.

"I'll make a bargain with you now!"
The wily King said, "If you vow
To fetch a Gorgon's head for me ~
Then I will set your mother free."

King Polydectes then decreed
That Perseus should do this deed
To prove to all that he deserved
To have the King keep to his word.

(Though everybody knew the task
Was quite beyond a mortal's grasp.)
The King was rubbing hands in glee ~
"While he is gone Danae's with me!"

Index: Painted Lady butterfly (Danae), Robber fly (Polydectes), 2 Stag beetles & 2 Hercules beetles(guards) Cockchafer (Perseus)

First Perseus should find out where
The Gorgon sisters had their lair.
To do this, he required to go
To three weird sisters, who should know
The Gorgon's cave, because you see
They're also sisters to those three.

These Graeae (that's what they were called)
Were rather frightful to behold:
Between the three of them to spy,
They passed around a single eye,
And eating meals was gross, in truth,
Because they only had one tooth.

Whilst Perseus was on his way
To meet the Graeae, and to slay
The Gorgon with the snakes for hair,
He found beside the path a pair
Of sandals which had wings, a sack,
A polished shield, and a hat;
And when he put the helmet on,
To his surprise he found he'd gone!
For it had made him disappear,
And seemingly, he wasn't there!

The sack was useful for the head
Of Gorgon, after she was dead,
And with his sword and brand new shield
He felt assured that she must yield.

(Now Hermes was the one who had
Left those winged sandals for the lad;
Then from the goddess Athene  
The shield, so he'd protected be;
And when in danger, if he wore 
The hat of Hades, to ensure
That he could creep about and be
Conferred invisibility,
He might survive this dreadful test.
Thus did the gods assist his quest.)

Index : Cave spiders, May bug (Cock chafer) (m)

So now all set for fighting he
Approached the Graeae sisters three.
He found them in their mountain den,
Brewing a ghastly stew, and when
They stirred the mixture in their urn,
And took the eye and tooth in turn,
He grabbed the eye as it was passed
Between them at their foul repast;
(Since Hades hat hid him from view
He'd snatched the eye before they knew
That they had company, which made
Them screech with fury) ~ and he bade
Them tell him where the Gorgons stay,
Or he would throw their eye away..........

"No! No!" they wailed, we CAN'T tell you,
We'll be in trouble if we do!
Kind sir, please do just give it back!
Oh woe is us, if we should lack
The means by which we all can see,
You wouldn't be so cruel, surely?"

But Perseus ignored their pleas,
E'en though they begged him on their knees,
'Till finally they wept and groaned,
And some directions they intoned.
He threw the eye down, and turned round,
To leave them groping on the ground,
And as he left, he heard them say ~

"He's good as dead now anyway!
For when he finds Medusa's home,

One glance will turn him into stone!"

48

Now the brave lad flies to find the homeland of the Gorgons,
Polished sheild and sword aloft, in case he meets a foe;
Keeping watch intently he soon spots the isle beneath him,
Rising up out of the sea that's foaming down below.

    Knowing that he mustn't see
                        Medusa's face directly,
  Hits upon a cunning plan to get into the hide:~
    Holding up his shield he inches slowly backwards,
                                standing
  Opposite the entrance to the cave where they're inside.

Index: Cockchafer, flat rock scorpions

                      Got her!
          He can see Medusa's head
                    in the reflection,
         She and both her sisters
    are all sleeping at that hour ~
      Snakes that hiss and writhe
about her head are always wakeful~
They will turn to stone all those who see her in her bower.
    But they cannot see him since he wears the hat of Hades,
  And, because he's flying in, they cannot hear his tread~
He is watching their reflection as he takes position~
With his sack kept open to receive Medusa's head.

Now he's moving in so
  he can be in striking distance,
Silently he's hovering
  whilst covering the ground ~

      SUDDENLY..........

SUDDENLY

..........................he swings his sword round,
      in a single movement ~
And it strikes Medusa's neck with
      a gut-wrenching sound.

She lets out a piercing shriek,
      then all around is chaos,
Gorgon sisters jerk awake,
      and leap into the fray,
But it is too late, the severed head
      has been wrapped tightly,
Perseus flies out of there.............
      and safely gets away.

So, having got Medusa's head
Young Perseus now homeward sped;
And as he crossed the desert sand
Some drips of blood began to land
Along a path which marked his track ~
For they were dripping from the sack;
And as they hit the ground they burned,
And into deadly vipers turned.

Then further on, he chanced to spy
Great Atlas, holding up the sky.
So, making sure his eyes were closed
He took the head out, and exposed
It to the giant, to arrange
Him as the Atlas mountain range.
Now turned to stone, his struggles o'er,
Into the skies those mountains soar.

Then, looking down, he saw with shock
A maiden chained upon a rock,
And flying down to rescue her
He heard her cry "LOOK OUT brave sir!"
He turned his head and saw a sight
Which made his blood run cold with fright ~
For from the waves a fearful beast
Was rising, to consume that feast
Which had been left out for it there
Upon that rock - the maiden fair.

Index: Cave scorpions, Cockchafer, Vipers, Bristletail

50

"Avert your eyes!" cried Perseus,
And took the head out of the purse;
The maiden and the lad were saved,
For, as it crashed in on the waves
The monster foul had turned to stone,
   Leaving the two of them alone.

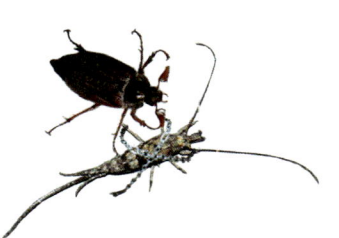

Then Perseus broke free her chain,
And took her back to land again,
And asked her father to explain
Just why he bound her to that chain,
Alone and naked out at sea,
A cruel fate for such as she.

"Brave sir," the King replied, "I know
That it was harsh to treat her so.
The great sea-god Poseidon sent
That monster as a punishment,
Because he chanced to overhear
My Queen the fair Kassiopeia
Declare she was more beautiful
Than his sea-nymphs in oceans cool,
Then, when the monster raged, we sought
Advice on how it could be fought;

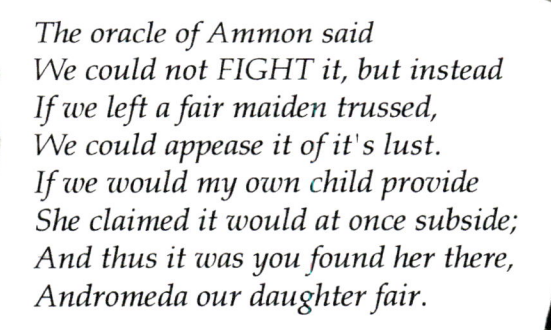

The oracle of Ammon said
We could not FIGHT it, but instead
If we left a fair maiden trussed,
We could appease it of it's lust.
If we would my own child provide
She claimed it would at once subside;
And thus it was you found her there,
Andromeda our daughter fair.

Now, since she owes to you her life,
You may take her to be your wife,
To show you we appreciate
Your saving her from that grim fate."

It seems she'd been bethrothed before
To one Phineus, who now swore
That she was going to be HIS bride
And Perseus should step aside.
(In spite of having first allowed
That she should die to save the crowd)

So, at the wedding feast he drew
His sword, to slay his rival, who
Just took out the Medusa's head ~
One look at that, and he was dead.

~~~~~~~~~~~~~~~~~~~~~~~~~~~~~~

Index : Cockchafer, Bristletail, Axolotl
             Cockroach

Author's note : For the purpose of the story I have the Axolotl turned to stone on the sea-shore. However Axolotls are amphibians which live in fresh-water. Some people keep them as pets.

51

Returning home, now Perseus
 Found Polydectes bent
On marrying Danae by force.
(Though she would not consent).
He challenged him, and said "I've brought
 Medusa's head for you!"
But Polydectes sneered and scoffed
 "That simply can't be true!"

So Perseus then shouted out "Who follows me, take heed!
Just turn your eyes away from me
 until my Mother's freed!"
Thus saying, he took out the head,
 and held it by the hair,

So all who looked on it were turned
 to stone as they stood there.

~~~~~~

Next, he returned the precious gifts which had been so much needed
In his success, and without which he couldn't have succeeded.
The hat, the shield, the flying shoes, to gods who had provided
These helpful aids, he swore to give allegiance undivided.

 The head of the dread gorgon he was very glad to yield
 To the great goddess Athene, to place upon her shield.

~~~~~~

 Then, hearing of the oracle that brought them to that land,
 Predicting that he'd some day kill his grandfather, he planned
 To travel PAST his place of birth, in case it should prove true,
 And entered some athletic games, as something he could do.

He demonstrated how to throw a quoit, which caught the wind,
And travelled far above the crowd - up and away it spinned.
Then, coming down at last, it hit the head of someone who
Was in that area by chance - he was just passing through.
They ran at once to see his fate, but found that he was dead.
The victim was his grandfather, just as the priestess said.

 And now the moral of this tale is plain for all to see ~~~~
 You cannot run away from fate, whate'er will be, will be.

SISYPHUS, King of Corinth

Now Sisyphus was not like us ~ his motives were more devious,
For he was full of trickery ~ (so *quite* unlike both you and me).
And Hades knew how slippery ~ a customer our S. could be ~
And so he came up person'ly ~ from Underworld, to oversee
The final journey of that soul ~ back to his kingdom down below.

He brought a pair of cuffs with him, ~ to bind that con-man full of sin,
So Sisyphus could not slip free: ~ "Your time is up! Now come with me!"
But Sisyphus, quite at his ease, ~ was cooking up another wheeze;
A plan that really was inspired ~ was what this circumstance required!
And so he artfully admired ~ the handcuffs Hades had acquired

"What fascinating novelties! ~ Do show me how you work them, please!"
Such weasel-words had cast their spell ~ on that great sov'reign lord of Hell,
And Hades, flattered, put them on, ~ to show that rogue how it was done.
Well, how naive can someone be! ~ He should have known, now shouldn't he?
And yes, you've guessed, our Sisyphus ~ ensnared the King and kept him trussed.

Well now all hell broke loose - the one ~ essential to the master-plan
That kept the spirit-world unharmed ~ had been most violently disarmed!
So no-one stood at Hades gate ~ to greet souls past their 'die-by' date,
For no-one died, and though they might ~ be chopped to bits ~ a horrid sight!
They just got up and walked away ~ to fight again another day!

It wasn't right! and finally ~ came rescuers to set him free.....
Released from his captivity ~ Hades was mad as he could be,
And promptly issued a decree: ~ "Make Sisyphus report to me!"
But once again that wily wretch ~ had schemed to get another stretch
Of dissipated life above, ~ with sunshine, merriment, and love.

Index: Dung beetle; Mole cricket

Before he died he told his wife ~ "When I have reached the end of life
Just keep my body lying round ~ do not inter it in the ground!"

Thus, since his body still remained ~ that rascal Sisyphus complained
To kindly Queen Persephone ~ "Your Highness, surely you can see
A *proper* funeral would be ~ appropriate for such as me?

Besides, I didn't have a coin ~ beneath my tongue, so I can't join
The dead folk on the other side ~ of River Styx! I hitched my ride
On Charon's ferry, that is why ~ I owe the fee, so I *can't* die
Until I've sorted out this mess ~ you must agree, your Graciousness?"

That oily scoundrel got away, ~ but when he reached the light of day
Forgot what he had said he'd do ~ to set the record straight and true,
And lived just as he had before ~ grim death came knocking at his door.

But even he could not escape ~ forever man's eventual fate,
And down in Hades once again ~ was forced to take his medicine:
"For crimes against the gods, you stand ~ condemned by all throughout this land;
And as a punishment, we say ~ that you must labour night and day."

His task ~ to roll a boulder up ~ a mountainside right to the top ~
Was pointless, for that wretched stone ~ had an agenda of it's own,
And all his efforts were in vain ~ because it rolled back down again!
And so he toils repeatedly ~ back down and up, eternally.
The trickster tricked! A cunning plan ~ to punish that most cunning man,

Thus Sisyphus, forced to atone ~ for all the evil he had done,
Sets an example of the way ~ that we might come to rue the day
If we decide to cheat and skive ~ and swindle, whilst we are alive.

Index: Dung beetle; Comma butterfly

THESEUS & THE MINOTAUR

King Minos was the fearsome king of Crete
    Queen Minos was the fearsome queen of Crete
Who gave his monster living flesh to eat.
    Who gave her monster living flesh to eat.
He terrorised the kingdoms round about –
    She terrorised the kingdoms round about –
They paid him tributes just to keep him out.
    They paid her tributes just to keep her out.

    The king of Athens used to send fourteen
    Young men and maidens to avoid his spleen.
    Young men and maidens to avoid her spleen

One year Prince Theseus, Aegeus' son
Said "Father, something really must be done!"
He vowed to go himself as one of those
Fourteen young men and maids Aegeus chose.
His father, King Aegeus, was aghast,
But Theseus to his brave plan stuck fast.

    So finally Aegeus told him "Son!
    The white sail will denote that it is done.
    I'll wait up on the cliff top every day
    And when I see your sail I'll shout "Hooray!"
    But if I see a black sail then I'll know
    That you have failed your quest to overthrow
    The Minotaur, that monster who devours
    So many of these men and maids of ours."

    So Theseus set sail and travelled to
      The court of Minos,
                with his faithful crew.
      When challenged
          to state who would be the first
    To slake the dreaded monster's
                     evil thirst
      For blood of living victims,
                  he stepped out,
      And cried,
           "I'll kill that Minotaur, no doubt!"

    "You boasting fool!
          Before this day is through
      My Minotaur will make
              mincemeat of you!"

    And with this threat the king
          had him cast down
    And with this threat the queen
          had him cast down
    Into the labyrinth beneath the ground.

Index: Bombadier beetles; queen meadow ant.

Author's note: Readers who prefer to be entomologically correct rather than mythologically correct should substitue 'Queen' for 'King' and 'she' for 'he'

But this cruel act had been observed by one
Who felt ashamed of what Minos had done.
Her heart beat faster as she gazed upon
That brave and handsome King of Athens' son.
The king's plain daughter then conceived a plan
The queen's plain daughter then conceived a plan
To save that reckless and courageous man.

So Ariadne (that's what she was called)
Crept to the crypt so dark and deep and walled.
She found brave Theseus had paused to stare
At all the tunnels he could follow there
And wonder which to choose to find the lair.
    So She called out to him "Psst! Over here!"

Then as he wandered over in a daze
"Unravel this as you go through the maze!"
She pressed a ball of thread into his hand
And put a sharpened sword in his waist band.
"You are a clever girl!" the Prince opined,
"When I get back we'll have to get entwined!"

So saying he set out and soon forgot
That Ariadne was part of this plot.
But Ariadne counted out the time
    And held on fast to her end of the twine.

    Meanwhile, our hero heard a roar, and ran
        Into his adversary, which began
            A battle which is famous to this day,
                For showing how a strategy can pay.

Our hero waved his sword about the air,   But Theseus was brave, and stood his ground,
The monster thrashed his tail and left his lair, And when the Minotaur began to pound
Then, lunging round the corridor so steep,   Toward him, he jumped up and grabbed his horn,
He chased our hero down into the deep   And twisted at his neck 'till it was torn,
Recesses of the labyrinth, and there   And plunged his sword into that deep neck vein
He had him cornered, gasping at stale air.   From which the blood of sacrifice may drain.

The monster groaned, and stamped, and tossed his head,
But Theseus hung on 'till he was dead,
And rolled him over with a mightly CRASH,
Which caused the rocks all round about to smash,
And echoed through the halls above their feet,
Where Minos' court had just sat down to eat.

Thus Minotaur, who was a MASSIVE beast,
Had met his end, and forfeited his feast,
And Theseus had lived to tell the tale,
And had a good escape route planned, as well.

~ ~

So he retraced his steps, re-winding thread
To guide him through that labyrinth so dread,
And at the door stood Ariadne who
Cried "I'm so glad that you have made it through!"

They freed the others, and together ran
Down to the harbour, where they all began
To sail for Athens. "Take me with you, please!"
The princess begged the Prince upon her knees,
"My Dad'll kill me, honestly he will!"
"My Mum'll kill me, honestly she will!"
(A cry which echoes down the ages still)

"Of course!" said Theseus, "Just jump aboard!"
And then he turned his mind to thoughts abroad.
"I must remember to change that black sail
To indicate to Pa I did prevail."

But, just before he did this he was pinned
By Ariadne, who stole all his wind
By saying "I'm so glad that I'm now free!
I'm out of here, and you will marry me!"

"I'll marry you!" the prince gasped out, appalled,
"That would be nice!" - and with such words he stalled
Her keen advances, 'till they reached some land
(The cunning prince had a fool's errand planned)

57

So Ariadne set off with a smile
To buy supplies from Naxos, a Greek isle.
Whilst she was doing this without a care,
He set sail with all haste to leave her there.

But in his hurry he forgot to change
That black sail for a white one, which was strange,
And proved to be a tragic oversight,
For King Aegeus watching from the height
Of cliff tops thought that he had failed the test,
And rent his clothes, and beat upon his breast.

Then in despair he threw himself into
The wide sea down below, so deep and blue.
And ever after that main came to be
Known to us all as the the Aegean Sea.

And so that old wives' tale still holds the clue
And 'Handsome is as handsome does' is true.

This handsome prince so vain, ungrateful too,
Had caused a lot of pain to those he knew,
And though he rid his people of the price
They paid in dues to Minos, 'twas not nice
Of Theseus to blithely use then shed
A maiden without whom he would be dead.

Thus by our actions everyone can see
What kind of people we've turned out to be.

C Diana Knight 2006

58

Greek name	Roman name	Roles	Photo taken by:

Where unstated Greek & Roman names are the same: Where unstated photos are by the author

ARACHNE		Victoria Steventon	
Athene (or Athena)	Minerva	Rona Knight	
Dionysus	Bacchus	Roland Knight	
		Leopard in Arachne's tapestry	Alex Knight
		Arachne's loom	Allen Crisp
ATALANTA		Long-legged fly (dolichopodidae)	
Hippomenes		Blow fly (Lucilian Caesar)	
DAPHNE		Cricket (Rosel's Metrioptera roeseli)	
& APOLLO		Broad-bodied chaser dragonfly (m)	Wikipedia
Eros	Cupid	Green shield bug	
		Laurel wreath	Wikipedia
DEMETER	Ceres	Comma butterfly	
& PERSEPHONE	Persipina	Comma butterfly	
Hades	Pluto	Mole cricket	David Element
Horse (pulling the chariot of Hades)		Devil's coach horse beetle	Simon Munnery
Zeus	Jupiter, Jove	Luber grasshopper	Grayce Dillon
Hermes	Mercury	Migrant hawker dragonfly	Joss Knight (3rd pic)
ECHO		Common lacewing	Simon Munnery
& NARCISSUS		Beautiful demoiselle	Simon Munnery (most pics)
Hera	Juno	Keeled skimmer dragonfly	Simon Munnery (1st pic)
HERACLES	Hercules	Toe-biter (large water bug)	From 'whatsthatbug' website
Hippolyte (human form)		Heath Roselli	
The golden hind		Bushcricket	Simon Munnery
Apollo		Broad-bodied chaser dragonfly (m)	David Element
Artemis		Broad-bodied chaser dragonfly (f)	David Element
Eurystheus		Wasp beetle	Simon Munnery
Augeias		Cardinal beetle	Simon Munnery
The cattle of the Augean stables		Nettle weevils	Simon Munnery
Orthus		Centipede(s)	
Minotaur (also pictured in 'ICARUS')		Thorny devil lizard	From Wikipedia by Eric R.Pianka
Diomedes		Green tiger beetle	Simon Munnery
The mares of Diomedes		Flesh flies	Simon Munnery
Hippolyte (insect form)		European hornet (vespa crabro)	Simon Munnery
Amazons		European hornets on nest	John Mason ardea@ardea
Geryon		Wolf spider	Simon Munnery
Eurytion the herdsman		Jewel beetle	Simon Munnery
Cerberus		Centipede(s)	Simon Munnery
ICARUS		Wood-ant	Unknown
Daedalus		Wood-ant	Unknown
		Mid-wife' ant and other meadow ants	David Element
		Large wood ant with tiny wood ant	Gary Skinner/Nature Portfolio
MIDAS		Emperor moth (m)	Owen Newman/osfimages
Pan	Faunus	Hoverfly	David Element
Apollo		Broad-bodied chaser dragonfly (m)	David Element
The barber		Praying mantis (f)	David Element
Faun		Long-horn beetle	David Element

**ORPHEUS
      & EURYDICE**
PANDORA('s box)
1st technician
2nd, 4th & 5th technician
3rd technician
Adam & Eve
Zeus
Epimetheus
Faith & Hope
Prometheus
Gaia

(pardoning)PROMETHEUS

PERSEUS
The Graeae (weird sisters)
The Gorgons
Andromeda
Kassiopeia   Cassiopeia

SISYPHUS

THESEUS
Atheneans
Ariadne
Minotaur

Cicada (Tibicen)
Tree hopper (both pictures)
Heath Roselli
Heath Roselli
Andrew Robertson
Yung-Yao Lin
Alex & Kathryn Knight
Rodney Knight
Kevin Morley
Madeleine Knight
Alex Knight
Heath Roselli
Golden eagle
Alex Knight
Most of the 'creatures'
Cock-chafer
Cave spiders
Rock scorpions
Bristletail

Vipers
Atlas mountains
Dung beetle
Mole cricket
Bombadier beetle
Bombadier beetles
Wood-ant
Thorny devil lizard

Dan Mozgai of cicadamania.com
Roger Key

Simon Munnery

Alex Knight
flying version from Wikipedia
Simon Munnery
Simon Munnery
Simon Munnery

Simon Munnery
Wikipedia
Shutterstock
David Element
From 'Bugguide' website
From 'Bugguide' website
from 'large wood-ant with tiny wood-ant'
From Wikipedia by Eric R.Pianka